Dear Parent:
Your child's love of reading

Every child learns to read in a different way
speed. Some go back and forth between rea   and read
favorite books again and again. Others read through each level in
order. You can help your young reader improve and become more
confident by encouraging his or her own interests and abilities. From
books your child reads with you to the first books he or she reads
alone, there are I Can Read Books for every stage of reading:

SHARED READING
Basic language, word repetition, and whimsical illustrations,
ideal for sharing with your emergent reader

BEGINNING READING
Short sentences, familiar words, and simple concepts
for children eager to read on their own

READING WITH HELP
Engaging stories, longer sentences, and language play
for developing readers

READING ALONE
Complex plots, challenging vocabulary, and high-interest topics
for the independent reader

I Can Read Books have introduced children to the joy of reading
since 1957. Featuring award-winning authors and illustrators and a
fabulous cast of beloved characters, I Can Read Books set the
standard for beginning readers.

A lifetime of discovery begins with the magical words **"I Can Read!"**

Visit www.icanread.com for information
on enriching your child's reading experience.

Magic Mixies Mixlings: Welcome to Mixia!
Copyright © 2023 The Moose Group. MAGIC MIXIES MIXLINGS™ logos, names
and characters are licensed trade marks of Moose Enterprises (INT) Pty Ltd.
All rights reserved. Printed in the United States of America.
No part of this book may be used or reproduced in any manner whatsoever without written permission
except in the case of brief quotations embodied in critical articles and reviews.
For information address HarperCollins Children's Books, a division of HarperCollins Publishers,
195 Broadway, New York, NY 10007.
www.icanread.com

ISBN 978-0-06-331088-9
Book design by Stephanie Hays

22 23 24 25 26   LB   10 9 8 7 6 5 4 3 2 1   First Edition

Welcome to Mixia!

Adapted by Mickey Domenici
Based on the episodes "Mixia" and "Vanishing Fiesta"
written by Katie Chilson

HARPER
An Imprint of HarperCollinsPublishers

Welcome to a magical world
hidden from humans.

It is full of dazzling surprises
and sparkly crystals.
Welcome to Mixia!

This is Sienna.

She is looking for some fun

in her Lolo's attic.

Lolo means grandpa.

She finds a magical crystal

that opens a door to Mixia.

Sienna is fearless.

She walks through the door.

★ Sienna ends up in a forest.
She finds a wand, spell book,
and cauldron.

Sienna decides to make a potion

to help find her way back home.

She collects the ingredients

and waves the wand.

Then she says, "Magicus Mixus!"

Suddenly a small creature appears.

Sienna created a Magic Mixie!

She names him Carrot.

A Mixie is a best pal and a guide.

Sienna asks Carrot how to get home.

Carrot knows the only place

with enough magic

to send Sienna home is the Castle.

But Sienna and Carrot get lost

on the way to the Castle.

Carrot tells Sienna to use

a cauldron to summon Mixlings.

12

He says Mixlings are magical beings
with cool powers like floating.
Carrot also has cool powers!
He can float.
Sienna uses a cauldron
to call two more Mixlings.

The first Mixling is Pixly.

Pixly may be small,

but her heart is big.

Pixly's power is casting charms.

When they ask her

how to get to the Castle,

Pixly happily leads the way.

She is one sweet Mixling!

15

The second Mixling is Geckler.

He has a really cool power.

He can make his hands glow!

When they get lost

in the dark Crystal Caves,

Geckler uses his hands to help

Sienna and Carrot find their way.

Finally, after finding their way
through the dark Crystal Caves,
the friends reach Mount Morph.
Mount Morph can change into anything,
like a castle or a waterfall!

Sienna uses a cauldron to summon

another Mixling to help.

She summons Luggle!

Just then Mount Morph's waterfall opens.

The friends head inside.

Uh-oh! The world turns upside down.

Sienna and her friends need to jump
and flip it around to set things right.
They jump and jump.
Wow, they did it!
Now let's go find the Castle.

Finally they reach Vanishing Vista.

Everyone is so tired.

A party will cheer them up!

Sienna wants to call more

Mixlings to help.

She finds a spell in the spell book.

Poof!

Let's meet the new Mixlings.
When the friends meet Parlo,
she seems a little grumpy!

Dawne is much sweeter.

She has wings and zips around.

She can soar above the clouds.

Time to get this party started!
Sienna and her new friends
set up for the party.
But—oh no—the decorations
and snacks start vanishing.

Sienna doesn't know what's happening.

She tries to cast a party-saving spell.

It covers everything in green goo!

The friends quickly discover

who is making

the snacks and decorations disappear.

It's Parlo!

It turns out her power

is turning invisible.

But the green goo makes Parlo visible.

Gotcha, Parlo!

The friends keep the party going.
And when the party is over,
Sienna, Carrot, and the Mixlings
will continue on their journey.

Someday it will be time
for Sienna to go home.
But now, the Castle is waiting,
and there are more adventures
to have in the world of Mixia!

Magicus Mixus!

Magic ingredients were hidden in the pages.

Can you find them all?